Dear Parents and Educators,

Welcome to Penguin Young Readers! As parents and educators, you know that each child develops at his or her own pace—in terms of speech, critical thinking, and, of course, reading. Penguin Young Readers recognizes this fact. As a result, each Penguin Young Readers book is assigned a traditional easy-to-read level (1–4) as well as a Guided Reading Level (A–P). Both of these systems will help you choose the right book for your child. Please refer to the back of each book for specific leveling information. Penguin Young Readers features esteemed authors and illustrators, stories about favorite characters, fascinating nonfiction, and more!

Bones and the Birthday Mystery

LEVEL **3**

GUIDED READING LEVEL **K**

This book is perfect for a **Transitional Reader** who:
- can read multisyllable and compound words;
- can read words with prefixes and suffixes;
- is able to identify story elements (beginning, middle, end, plot, setting, characters, problem, solution); and
- can understand different points of view.

Here are some **activities** you can do during and after reading this book:
- Creative Writing: Have the child pretend he/she is going to the circus with Bones, Grandpa, and Sally. What would he/she like to do at the circus? What would he/she eat? Which shows would he/she see?
- Reading with Expression: Although many transitional readers can read text accurately, they may read slowly or not smoothly and pay little or no attention to punctuation. One way to improve this is to read out loud. For example, read pages 24 and 25 in this story aloud. Have the child pay special attention to how your voice changes when you come to different punctuation marks, such as commas, periods, or exclamation points. Then have the child read a different page out loud to you.

Remember, sharing the love of reading with a child is the best gift you can give!

—Bonnie Bader, EdM
 Penguin Young Readers program

*Penguin Young Readers are leveled by independent reviewers applying the standards developed by Irene Fountas and Gay Su Pinnell in *Matching Books to Readers: Using Leveled Books in Guided Reading*, Heinemann, 1999.

To Rachelli, Tzippora, Ayelet, Yakira,
and Aharon—DA

For Harry and Gloria. You guys rock—BJN

Penguin Young Readers
Published by the Penguin Group
Penguin Group (USA) Inc., 375 Hudson Street, New York, New York 10014, USA
Penguin Group (Canada), 90 Eglinton Avenue East, Suite 700, Toronto, Ontario M4P 2Y3, Canada
(a division of Pearson Penguin Canada Inc.)
Penguin Books Ltd, 80 Strand, London WC2R 0RL, England
Penguin Ireland, 25 St Stephen's Green, Dublin 2, Ireland (a division of Penguin Books Ltd)
Penguin Group (Australia), 707 Collins Street, Melbourne, Victoria 3008, Australia
(a division of Pearson Australia Group Pty Ltd)
Penguin Books India Pvt Ltd, 11 Community Centre, Panchsheel Park, New Delhi—110 017, India
Penguin Group (NZ), 67 Apollo Drive, Rosedale, Auckland 0632, New Zealand
(a division of Pearson New Zealand Ltd)
Penguin Books (South Africa), Rosebank Office Park, 181 Jan Smuts Avenue,
Parktown North 2193, South Africa
Penguin China, B7 Jiaming Center, 27 East Third Ring Road North,
Chaoyang District, Beijing 100020, China

Penguin Books Ltd, Registered Offices: 80 Strand, London WC2R 0RL, England

Text copyright © 2007 by David A. Adler. Illustrations copyright © 2007 by Barbara Johansen Newman.
All rights reserved. First published in 2007 by Viking and in 2009 by Puffin Books, imprints of
Penguin Group (USA) Inc. Published in 2013 by Penguin Young Readers, an imprint of
Penguin Group (USA) Inc., 345 Hudson Street, New York, New York 10014. Manufactured in China.

The Library of Congress has cataloged the Viking edition
under the following Control Number: 2006003511

ISBN 978-0-14-241432-3   10 9 8 7 6

BONES

and the **Birthday** Mystery

by David A. Adler

illustrated by Barbara Johansen Newman

Penguin Young Readers

An Imprint of Penguin Group (USA) Inc.

Contents

Chapter 1
Plop! Plop!

"It's hot! It's hot!" Dad said.

He took a large cake from the oven.

He put it on the table.

It smelled so good!

"Don't taste it," Dad said.

"It's for Grandpa's party."

Mom was making the icing.

"When the cake is cool," Mom said,

"you can ice it."

I waited.

I touched the cake.

It was still hot.

I waited and waited until it was cool.

"Hey, Mom.

Hey, Dad.

May I take a tiny taste?

I'll cover it with icing.

No one will know."

Mom looked at Dad.

"Okay," Mom said,

"but just a tiny taste."

I took a tiny piece off the side.

Mmm!

I took another tiny piece.

Mom gave me the bowl of icing.

I took a large spoon.

I filled it with icing

and held it over the cake.

Plop! Plop!

Icing fell onto the top of the cake.

I spread it around.

I turned the cake on its side.

I held up another spoonful of icing.

Plop! Plop!

Icing fell onto the side of the cake.

I spread it around.

I did that lots of times

until the cake was covered.

The table, my chair,

my shirt, and my hands

were covered with icing, too.

I wondered if Grandpa would know

that I tasted his cake.

I took out my glass.

I looked at the cake.

The missing piece was covered.

"Hey," I said.

"The missing piece is missing!"

I always know when something

is missing.

I'm a detective.

My name is Bones,

Detective Jeffrey Bones.

I find clues.

I solve mysteries.

Chapter 2
I'm Not Uncle Fester

"Let's go," Dad said.

He took the cake.

Mom gave me the birthday card.

"It's Grandpa's gift," she said.

"A card is not a good gift," I said.

Mom said, "It's more than a card."

I knew what to do.

I'm a detective.

I held it up to the light

and looked through the envelope.

I only saw a card.

"Let's go," Dad said again.

I took my detective bag.

I always take it.

A good detective

must always be ready

to solve a mystery.

I sat in the back of the car.

Dad put the cake next to me.

Mom drove awhile.

Then she stopped.

"Hey," I said.

"Grandpa doesn't live here."

"It's Sally's house," Mom said.

"We're taking her
to Grandpa's party."

Sally is Grandpa's friend.

She's nice.

Dad put the cake on my lap.

There was icing on the seat.

Dad wiped it off.

Sally sat in the back, next to me.

She had a big box on her lap.

It was wrapped and had a ribbon.

It was a gift for Grandpa.

When we got to Grandpa's house,

Dad took the cake.

Mom was about to ring the bell.

"Wait!" I said.

I took a fake beard, old hat,

and funny eyeglasses

from my detective bag

and put them on.

I rang the bell.

Grandpa opened the door.

He said, "Hello,"

to Mom, Dad, and Sally.

He looked at me and asked,

"And who are you?"

"Guess," I said.

"Uncle Fester?"

"No."

"Cousin Meko?"

"No."

I took off the beard,

hat, and eyeglasses.

"It's me," I said.

We hugged.

Then we went inside.

17

Lots of Grandpa's friends were there.

Dad gave Grandpa the cake
and said, "This is for you."
Sally gave Grandpa the box.
Mom said, "Jeffrey has a gift
to give you.
It's a great gift.
Hey," Mom asked me,
"where's Grandpa's birthday card?
Where's Grandpa's gift?"

Chapter 3
It's a Surprise!

"Was it in a big box?" Fred asked.

Fred is Grandpa's friend.

"No," Mom said.

"It was in an envelope
with a birthday card."

"What fits in an envelope?"

Jane asked.

She's Grandpa's friend, too.

"A small green picture of President Lincoln would fit," Fred said.

"The gift isn't money," Mom said.

Fred said, "Maybe it's a Willie Mays baseball card. I saw him play."

"No," Dad said.

"It's not a baseball card."

"Then what is it?" Sally asked.

"It's a surprise," Mom said.

"Well, I'll find it," I said.

"I'm a detective

and detectives find things."

I reached into my detective bag.

I took out my detective pen and pad.

I asked Mom when she last saw

Grandpa's birthday card.

"I gave it to you," Mom said.

She was right.

I wrote my name—*Jeffrey Bones*—

on my detective pad.

"Maybe it's in the car," I said.

We all went to the car.

The card wasn't there.

"Maybe Jeffrey left it at home,"
Dad said.

"Let's go there and look," Mom said.

I told everyone,

"I'll find Grandpa's gift."

"I know you will," Grandpa said.

Before Mom, Dad, and I left,

I whispered to Grandpa,

"Please, save some cake for me."

Grandpa said he would.

Chapter 4
I Solved the Mystery!

The kitchen was a mess.

Icing was everywhere.

We looked in the dish closet

and under the table

for Grandpa's birthday card.

I took out my detective pen and pad.

Table, I wrote on my pad.

I touched the icing on the table.

Sticky icing, I wrote on my pad.

I tasted the icing.

Yummy, I wrote.

I put my pad down

and ate more icing.

"It's not here," Mom said.

"Let's go."

My hand stuck

to the detective pad.

The detective pad stuck to the table.

Dad said to me,

"It's too bad

we lost Grandpa's gift.

It was really a gift

for you and Sally, too."

A gift for me!

I thought about the birthday card.

Mom gave it to me

when I was in

the house.

In the car, I looked at the clues.

Jeffrey Bones, *Table*,

Sticky icing, and *Yummy*.

I looked at my detective pad.

It was stuck to me again.

"Sticky icing!

That's it!"

I told Mom and Dad.

"I know where to find Grandpa's card.

I solved the mystery."

Chapter 5
You'll See

"Where is it?" Mom and Dad asked.

"It's at Grandpa's," I said.

"But we looked," Mom said.

"We looked everywhere."

"No we didn't," I said.

I thought about the gift.

Dad said it was

for me and Sally, too.

"What's Grandpa's gift?" I asked.

"Is it really for me, too?"

"You'll see," Dad said.

When we got to Grandpa's house,

Grandpa, Sally, Fred, and Jane asked,

"Did you find the card?

Did you find the gift?"

The cake was still on the table.

Grandpa hadn't cut it.

He had waited for me.

"Your card was never lost," I said.

"Dad already gave it to you."

"He did?" Grandpa asked.

"I did?" Dad asked.

"I iced the cake," I said.

Mom said, "You iced your shirt
and pants, too."

"There was icing everywhere," I said.

"Even on the bottom of the cake plate.

"Grandpa's card was on my lap.

Dad put the cake on my lap.

The card stuck

to the bottom of the plate."

Grandpa looked under the cake plate,

and there it was.

I had solved the mystery.

Grandpa opened the envelope
and read the card.
Then he showed us all

Mom and Dad's gift—
three tickets to the circus.
One ticket was for Grandpa.

One was for Sally,
and one was for me.
"I love the circus," I said.

Grandpa and Sally said
they love the circus, too.

We sang to Grandpa.

Then he cut the cake.

Even before he gave me a piece,

I knew I would love that, too.